Tomie de Paola's
KITTEN KIDS™
and the Missing Dinosaur

A GOLDEN BOOK · NEW YORK

Western Publishing Company, Inc., Racine, Wisconsin 53404

© 1988 by The Philip Lief Group, Inc. All rights reserved. Printed in the U.S.A. by Western Publishing Company, Inc. Produced by The Philip Lief Group, Inc. Graphics Studio for The Philip Lief Group, Inc.: R&D Productions, Inc. No part of this book may be reproduced or copied in any form without written permission from the publisher. GOLDEN®, GOLDEN & DESIGN®, and A GOLDEN BOOK® are trademarks of Western Publishing Company, Inc. Library of Congress Catalog Card Number: 87-81926 ISBN: 0-307-10613-6/ISBN: 0-307-60613-9 (lib. bdg.)   A B C D E F G H I J K L M

Kitten Kids™ is a trademark of The Philip Lief Group, Inc.

"Kit, it's time for your nap," Mama called.

"I'm too big to take a nap," complained Kit. Each day he explained to Mama that he didn't need a nap anymore. And each day Mama smiled and said, "Soon."

Kit went to his room and climbed onto his bed. Even though he knew he was too big to take a nap, his animal friends still got tired in the afternoon. Kit didn't really mind keeping them company.

Kit looked around. Something seemed odd to him—the animals looked different, somehow.

"Good night, Owl, and Unicorn, and Old Bear," he said.

Before he could figure out what was wrong, Kit was slipping off to sleep.

Suddenly Kit heard voices. "I must be dreaming,"
he thought.

"Where did she go?" Unicorn asked.

"I hope she's okay," added Owl.

"I think we should tell Kit," said Old Bear, in a very
serious voice.

Kit rubbed his eyes and sat up. "Tell Kit what?" he asked.

"Little Stegosaurus is missing," explained Owl. "We don't know where she is."

"So that's what's wrong!" said Kit. "I knew something had happened."

"We'd better try to find her," said Owl.

"Perhaps she went back to the toy store," said Old Bear.

"I think she went looking for other dinosaurs!" said
Owl. "Last night, when I was talking about my cousin
Barn Owl, Little Stegosaurus said she wished she could
meet some of her cousins."

"I know where we can find her cousins," said Kit.
"We have to go back to the time of the dinosaurs. And I
know just how to do it!

"Last week, Katie and I made this time machine," Kit continued. "It can take us into the future, or back into the past."

"How does it work?" asked Old Bear.

"It's easy," said Kit. "You just step inside it, close your eyes, think hard about the time you want to travel to, and count to five."

"That *is* easy," said Owl. "Let's go!"

They all got into the time machine, thought hard, and closed their eyes.

"One, two, three, four, five," counted Kit. "Okay, everybody. Open your eyes!" said Kit.

There they were—right in the land of dinosaurs.

Thump! Scrunch! Thump! Before them stood the biggest animal they had ever seen.

"Who are you?" asked Kit.

"I'm Triceratops," was the answer. "And who are you? You don't look like anything I've seen around here before." Triceratops looked curiously at Unicorn. "That's a very pretty horn you have there," she said. "I wonder if we're related."

"I don't think so," said Unicorn. "We don't live here. We're just looking for our friend Little Stegosaurus. Have you seen her?"

"Well," said Triceratops, "I saw a very little Stegosaurus early this morning over by the water."

"Owl, fly over there and see what you can find," suggested Kit, and off Owl went.

Owl heard a voice call from a tree. "Hey, you!" it said. "You're not an Archaeopteryx like me. I've never seen anything like you up here before."

"Hello," said Owl. "I'm trying to find my friend Little Stegosaurus. Have you seen her?"

"There's a baby Stegosaurus right over there." Archaeopteryx pointed. "I don't know if it's your friend, though."

Owl flew back to get the others. But much to their surprise, the Stegosaurus they found didn't look like a baby at all. It was enormous.

"Excuse me," said Kit. "Have you seen a little Stegosaurus?"

"I am the littlest Stegosaurus around here," was the reply. "Is someone looking for me?"

"Oh, no," said Kit. "We are looking for a very little Stegosaurus." He held up his hands to show the size.

"That's ridiculous!" said the Stegosaurus. "Maybe she's not a Stegosaurus at all. Does this baby have beautiful plates on her back like mine?"

"She does," said Old Bear, "and she has the loveliest blue fur."

"Blue fur!" said the Stegosaurus. He laughed until the ground shook.

Kit, Owl, Unicorn, and Old Bear looked everywhere.

The frisky Allosaurus had not seen Little
Stegosaurus.

The ferocious Tyrannosaurus had not seen Little Stegosaurus. No one they met had seen Little Stegosaurus anywhere.

Kit was very sad. He knew it was time to go home. By now it would be time for him to get up from his nap, and Mama would be looking for him.

"I don't think we'll find Little Stegosaurus here
anyway," said Owl wisely.
And so they headed home, just the way they had come.

They were barely back on Kit's bed when Kit heard
Katie calling him. Then Katie ran into the room.
"Are you up?" she asked.

In her hand was Little Stegosaurus.
"I borrowed your dinosaur," she said. "I wanted to show her to my friend Katrina."

"You took her?" asked Kit excitedly. "You didn't even ask!"

"I didn't think you would mind. I thought you'd be sleeping. Anyway, I brought her back," said Katie.

Kit looked at Owl, Unicorn, and Old Bear. He expected them to be very upset with Katie.

But they didn't look angry at all. They just looked happy to have Little Stegosaurus back with them, right where she belonged.